P9-BZI-102

# Alien Invaders

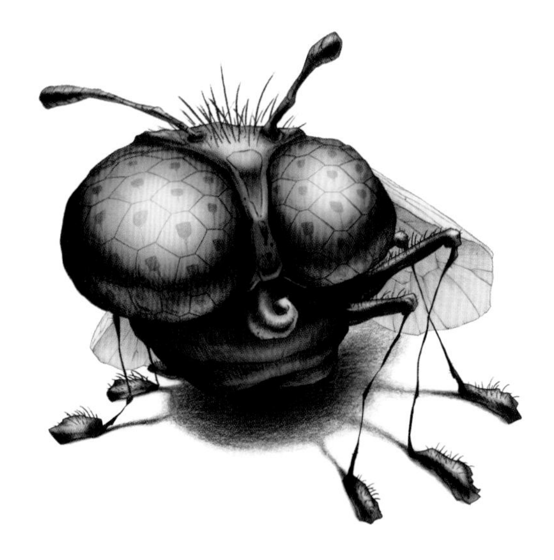

Written by Lynn Huggins-Cooper
Illustrated by Bonnie Leick

For Alex, Bethany, Eleanor—
and all the happy hours spent bug hunting!
—Lynn Huggins-Cooper

**For my family, my friends, and all the bugs I encountered in my youth.**
**—Bonnie Leick**



Huggins-Cooper, Lynn.

Alien invaders / written by Lynn Huggins-Cooper; illustrated by Bonnie Leick;
—1st ed.—McHenry, IL : Raven Tree Press, 2010.

p.;cm.

SUMMARY: A child compares garden creatures to what he knows of space invaders. Bugs and creepy crawlers abound in far–out illustrations.

English-only Edition
ISBN: 978-1-934960-83-7 hardcover

Bilingual Edition
ISBN: 978-0-9724973-9-8 hardcover
ISBN: 978-0-9741992-7-6 paperback

Audience: pre-K to 3rd grade
Title available in English-only or bilingual English-Spanish editions

1. Insects—Juvenile fiction. 2. Gardens—Juvenile fiction.
3. Imagination—Juvenile fiction. 4. Life on other planets—Juvenile fiction. I. Illust. Leick, Bonnie. II. Title.

LCCN: 2003109087

Printed in Taiwan
10 9 8 7 6 5 4 3 2 1
First Edition

**Free activities for this book are available at www.raventreepress.com**

# Alien Invaders

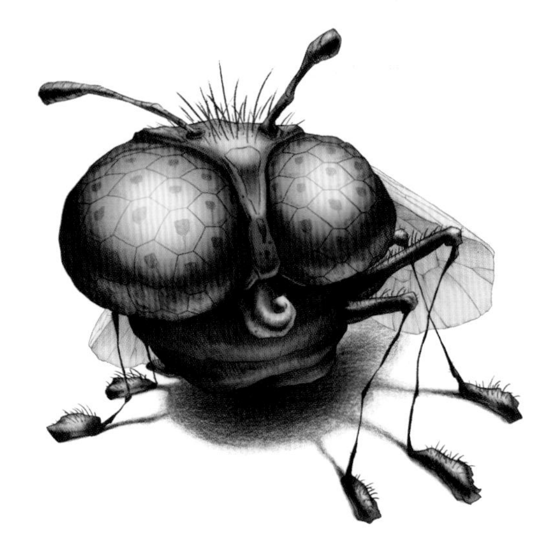

Written by Lynn Huggins-Cooper
Illustrated by Bonnie Leick

I heard that aliens are little green men.

Wrong!

The alien invaders are here.

**They set up camp in our garden.**

They have robot legs.

They wear shiny suits and helmets.

They watch us
with camera-lens eyes.

Are they taking pictures?

Some fly and dive.

**Others slither.**

**They leave clues.**

I hear them whisper
in secret languages.

I see them dance
strange dances.

They build cities
under our feet...

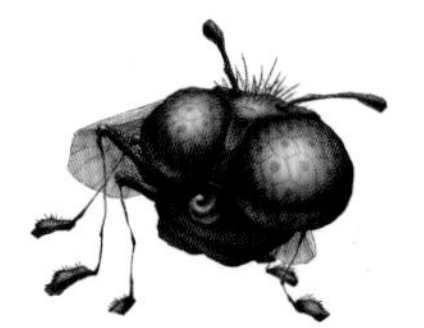

and spin
dangerous traps.

They sneak
into our houses
and watch us.

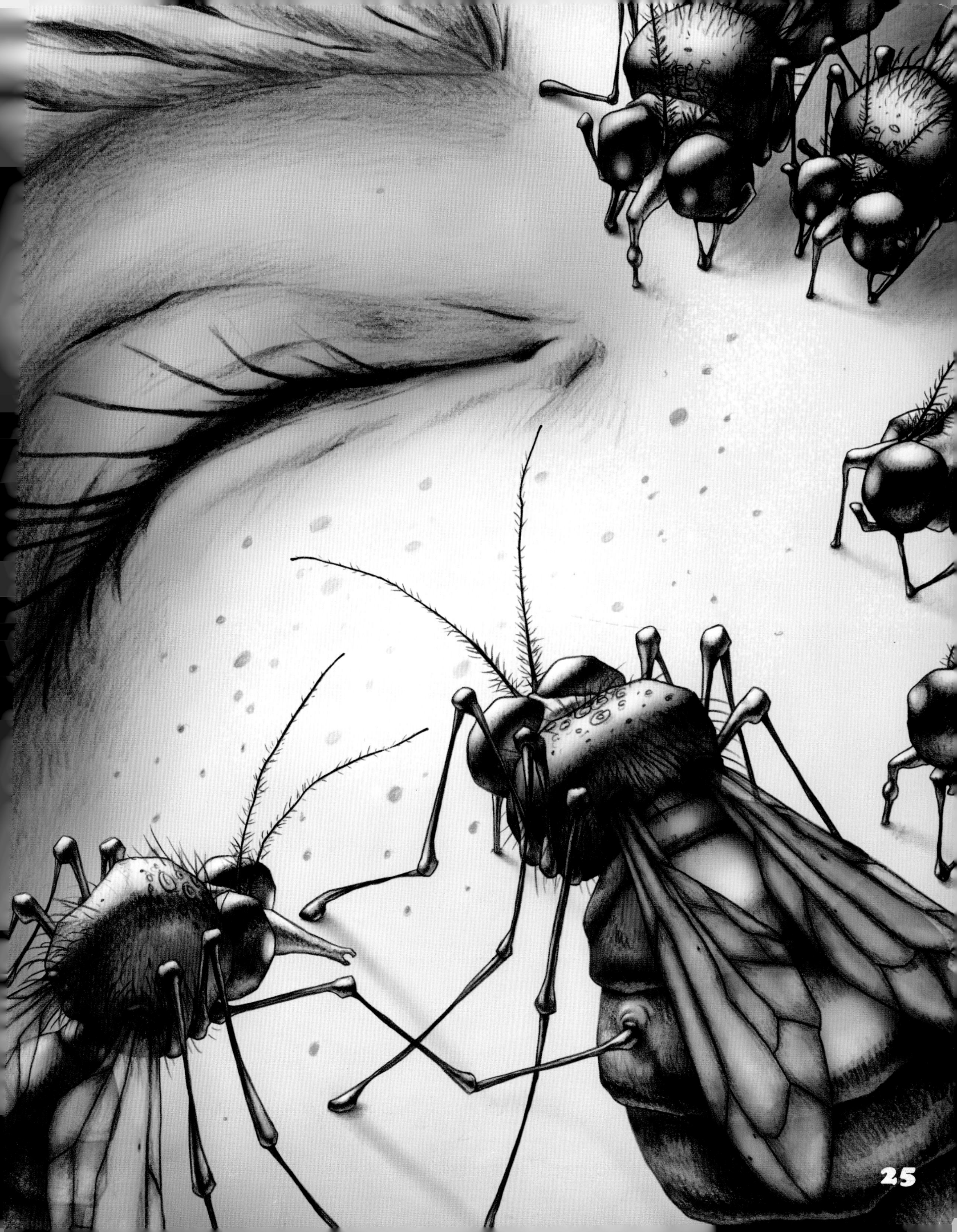

There are many
more of them
than us.

Mom says they are just bugs.

But I am making friends with them, just in case.

They sure look like aliens to me!

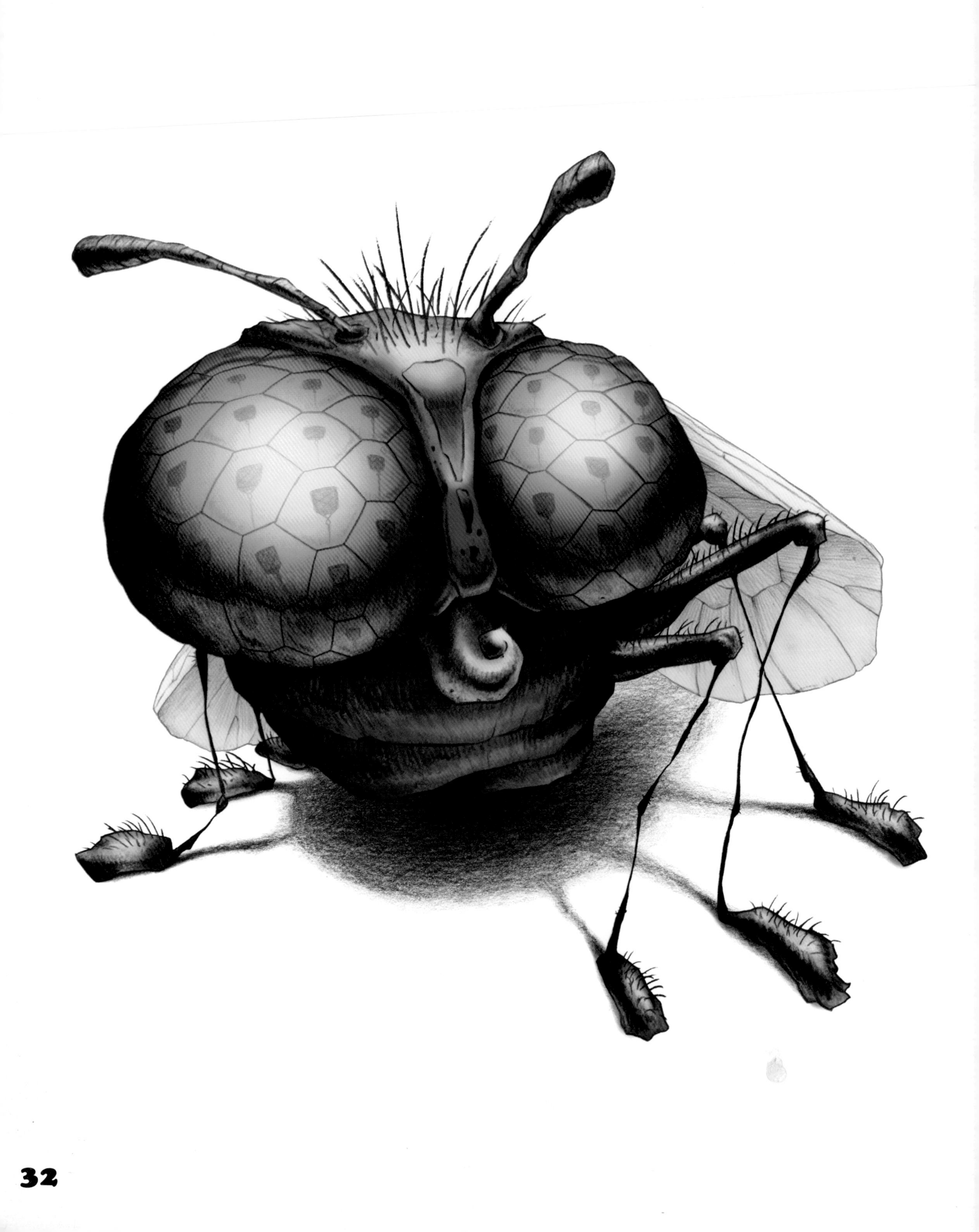